Scholastic Children's Books
An imprint of Scholastic Ltd
Euston House, 24 Eversholt Street, London, NW1 1DB, UK
Registered office: Westfield Road, Southam, Warwickshire, CV47 0RA
SCHOLASTIC and associated logos are trademarks and/or
registered trademarks of Scholastic Inc.

First published in the UK by Scholastic Ltd, 2017

Trade ISBN 978 1407 17079 4
Book Club ISBN 978 1407 17431 0

A CIP catalogue record for this book
is available from the British Library.

Printed by CPI Group (UK) Ltd, Croydon, CR0 4YY

Papers used by Scholastic Children's Books are made
from wood grown in sustainable forests.

1 3 5 7 9 10 8 6 4 2

This is a work of fiction. Names, characters, places, incidents
and dialogues are products of the author's imagination or are used
fictitiously. Any resemblance to actual people, living or dead,
events or locales is entirely coincidental.

www.scholastic.co.uk

Tiara Friends

The Mystery of the Lake Monster

Paula Harrison

SCHOLASTIC

*For my dad, who always
chased the monsters away*

Chapter One
Jax Makes Mischief

Princess Amelia (who was called Millie, for short) raced down the servants' corridor of Peveril Palace. Her satin dress swished around her legs and her pretty yellow shoes clattered on the stone floor. "Jess!" she called. "Wait for me!"

Jess, a palace maid, swung round and grinned. She had a little white apron fastened over her black uniform and her mob cap sat crookedly on her golden-brown hair. "Quick, Millie! We have to swap before they notice we've gone."

Millie sped up, nearly skidding on the smooth floor. Steadying herself, she gazed into the kitchen where Cook Walsh was bustling around the stove. It was only two days till the Peveril Palace Festival and Cook had been working from sunrise to sunset all week baking pies and cakes for the competitions.

Millie longed to go and help but princesses weren't supposed to get their clothes covered in jam and flour. She breathed in deeply, enjoying the delicious cooking smells drifting into the passageway. "Mm, cherry pie!" she murmured.

"Come on or they'll catch us!" said Jess, laughing, and she grabbed her friend's hand. Together they ran to the end of the passage,

slipped into Jess's chamber and closed the
door behind them.

Jess and Millie had known each other
since they were babies and they'd been best
friends ever since Jess came to work as a
maid at Peveril Palace.

The two girls were the same height and the same age (although Millie liked to remind Jess that she was ten days older). They both had glossy brown hair with golden tints that curled over their shoulders, and they both had rosy cheeks and hazel eyes. They were almost identical, except that Jess's eyes were slightly darker.

Leaning against the door, Millie tried to catch her breath. She and Jess had the most amazing secret: they shared clothes and swapped places with each other all the time! No one ever noticed that Jess became Millie and Millie turned into Jess because they looked so alike.

Millie smiled. Having a best friend that looked the same was Very Handy Indeed. She and Jess often swapped places to do the things they liked the most. Jess would take Millie's horse-riding lesson while Millie went to bake cakes with Cook Walsh. The kindly, grey-haired cook was the only person who knew their secret and she'd promised never to tell.

Swapping places had become extra handy because mysterious things had started happening in Plumchester. First, a crown had been stolen from the palace and then a silk dress had gone missing from Jess's parents' shop in Bodkin Street. The girls had turned detective to solve these puzzles. It had been great fun!

"We got away at last!" said Millie. "I was starting to think Mr Larum would never let me go. This morning he made me practise one hundred spellings." She pulled a face. Mr Larum, her teacher, was a kind man but he was very serious sometimes.

"Mr Steen said he doesn't want the guests to see a single speck of dust while they're here," groaned Jess. "He made me polish the candlesticks ten times!"

Mr Steen was the royal butler and liked everything to be shiny and perfect. Now that important guests had come to stay, he wanted everything even cleaner and shinier than usual.

The visiting lords and ladies had come to see the festival which was held every year on the palace lawn. In two days' time, the people of Plumchester would troop through the gates of Peveril Palace and set up stalls of fruit and vegetables as well as cakes, pies and jam. There would be games, singing and dancing too. Prizes would be given out for the very best thing on each stall. Cook Walsh was determined to win first prize for the pies and cakes of course!

Footsteps sounded in the corridor. Millie crouched down and put her eye to the keyhole. "It's Mr Steen." She watched the lanky butler prowl down the corridor in his black suit and white gloves. Every few seconds he paused and held a large round glass to his eye. "He's using his magnifying glass," she whispered. "I wonder what he's up to."

"I bet he's searching for dust," muttered Jess.

Millie put her hand over her mouth to stop a giggle escaping. At last she straightened up, her eyes sparkling. "He's gone now! Are you ready to swap?"

"Ready!" Jess nodded her head so energetically that her mob cap fell off.

Millie took off her yellow satin dress while Jess pulled off her maid uniform. Underneath they were both wearing cotton slips that looked like thin white dresses. Jess handed the maid clothes to Millie, and Millie gave the satin dress to Jess. A moment later they were wearing each other's clothes.

"Just one more thing!" Jess popped her white mob cap on Millie's head and tied up her own hair with her friend's yellow ribbon.

Millie looked in the little, square mirror that hung on the wall. No one would guess she was a princess now! "I'm going to see if Cook wants any help with those cakes."

"I'm going to visit the horses!" said Jess.

Opening the door a little, the girls peeked out. The corridor was empty.

"Meet you back here later!" Millie held out her little finger and Jess linked her pinkie with Millie's. This was their secret sign that they were best friends.

"See you later, Double Trouble!" Jess grinned before slipping out of the back door into the stable yard.

Millie hurried towards the kitchen, stopping when she heard a torrent of barking at the far end of the passage. It must be Jax, her golden cocker spaniel. Millie's heart sank. She hoped he wasn't getting into trouble again.

Holding her mob cap to her head, Millie dashed down the passageway. All the very important guests, who were staying to see the festival, were gathered in the entrance hall.

The Duke and Duchess of Sherbourne, a short couple with grey hair, were talking quietly. Lady Snood, a thin woman in a frilly dress, was checking her face in the hall mirror. Lord Dellwort, a dark-eyed man with a silky moustache, stood watching everyone.

Barking broke out again from inside the State Room.

"This dog needs proper training!" Millie heard her father, King James, say sharply. "Where is Mr Steen? Find him at once, please."

A palace guard ran out of the State Room. "Has anyone seen the butler?"

Millie hurried past him. Her father loved animals but he didn't like it when Jax got overexcited. "It's all right – I can help," she told the guard as she went inside.

King James was taking a shiny silver key out of a wooden desk. Marching across the room, he unlocked the Royal Jewel Cabinet and let its glass door swing open. The Jewel Cabinet was the place where all the most precious royal things were kept. The shelves were filled with masses of bracelets, tiaras, shiny goblets and crystal glasses.

Jax was gambolling round the room, his floppy ears swinging. Every now and then, he bounced up to Millie's father and gave the king's velvet robe a playful tug.

"Stop it, Jax!" Millie pulled her mob cap down low, hoping that her father wouldn't notice it was her wearing the maid dress. She caught hold of Jax. The spaniel gave a woof of delight and licked her hand.

"Oh, thank goodness!" said the king. "I've never seen him act so naughty."

"He must need a walk." Millie crouched down, rubbing Jax's fluffy coat. "I'll take him outside right now."

"It's all right, everybody!" the king called to his guests. "Come in and I'll show you the goblet I was talking about."

The duke and duchess, Lady Snood and Lord Dellwort, trooped in. King James picked up a gleaming golden cup. "This was given to my grandfather by Queen Isidora of Plutenburg more than a hundred years ago. The gold was mined from beneath the Trummel Mountains."

"Yes, very nice!" Lady Snood dismissed the goblet with a wave of her hand. "But what's that shiny blue necklace at the back?"

"You mean this one?" King James put down the goblet and took out a beautiful blue stone shaped like a teardrop which hung from a gold chain. "This is the famous Sky Sapphire named for its wonderful light blue colour. Most sapphires are quite a dark blue but not this one! It's the largest jewel in the whole kingdom and I gave it to Queen Belinda on our wedding day."

"What a lovely gift," said the Duchess of Sherbourne. "I bet it's worth a lot of money."

"All jewellery looks the same to me!" said Lord Dellwort, yawning.

Jax gave a short bark. Millie suddenly remembered she was supposed to be taking him for a walk, not staring at the jewel cabinet. As she hurried the spaniel out of the room, she caught sight of Lady Snood reaching out to touch the sapphire necklace.

Millie saw the lady's expression darken as the king put the jewel away. Her elegant eyes narrowed and her pale forehead scrunched into a frown. Millie remembered that stare as she bundled Jax outside. Lady Snood looked as if she wanted the Sky Sapphire all for herself.

Chapter Two

The Eyes in the Mist

Millie clipped Jax's lead to his collar and took him past the guard at the palace door. Jax's ears pricked up and he wagged his tail as they set off across the grass. Mist hung in the air like a pale curtain making it difficult to see very far.

Millie looked around for Jess. She was probably still in the stables petting the horses, or gathering apples in the orchard.

"Woof!" barked Jax, pulling on the lead.

"All right – I'll hurry up!" Millie laughed, letting the spaniel pull her past the tall hedges of the maze. She kept a tight hold on his lead as they passed the vegetable garden. Last week he'd trampled over rows of cabbages and Mr Polly, the head gardener, had got really cross.

Many of the vegetables Cook used in the palace kitchen were grown in this garden by the orchard. The round purple tops of the turnips peeped out of the ground next to rows of feathery-leaved carrots. Behind the carrots were rows of fat pumpkins and potato plants.

As soon as they'd passed the vegetable plot, Millie unclipped the lead and Jax hurtled across the grass in the direction of the lake. Millie ran after him but the golden-haired dog was soon swallowed up by the mist. "Jax!" she called. "Wait for me!"

"Millie!" Jess dashed up to her, bits of hay clinging to her yellow dress. "I thought you'd be in the kitchen making pies."

"Jax was being naughty so I brought him out for a walk," Millie explained, scanning the mist up ahead. It was so thick she couldn't even see the lake at the bottom of the slope.

There was a distant splash.

"I bet that's Jax trying to make friends with the ducks again!" Jess raced down the hill. "Jax! Come back!"

Millie ran after her. "Jax! Come here, boy."

They stopped at the lake shore and gazed at the mist swirling above the water.

"Jax! Where are you?" Millie's voice echoed. She stopped, listening for a bark or rustling in the bushes nearby, but there was silence.

Millie shivered. There was something a little creepy about the mist and how it hid things from view. "It's so quiet! Shall we split up to try and find him?"

"Good idea! I'll go to the bridge and you look by the boathouse," said Jess. "I'm sure he can't be far away."

Just then, there was a terrible shriek. Millie edged backwards, nearly tripping over a bramble.

"Oh my goodness!" gasped Jess. "Who was that?"

"There's a monster!" squealed a girl. "A monster in the water!" Then footsteps quickened like the pounding of a drum.

"That's Connie!" said Millie, recognizing the older girl's voice. "She must be on the bridge."

Together, Millie and Jess raced along the bank. They reached the bridge just as Connie, another palace maid, scuttled across. Her face was pink and her eyes were wide with fright.

"Connie, are you all right?" asked Jess.

The older girl clutched the railing at the side of the bridge. Her shoulders heaved as she struggled to get her breath back. "There's a monster right there in the water!" she gasped. "Its eyes ... they were so terrible and black! And its mouth was so wide!" She gave a shudder and then ran on towards the palace.

Millie and Jess exchanged horrified glances. Connie usually acted like they were too young for her to talk to. They'd never seen her in a panic before.

"How can there be a monster?" said Jess. "I've never seen anything like that in the lake."

"She looked pretty scared though." Millie peered at the green-blue water.

"That's true!" Jess stepped away from the bridge. "Maybe we should come back and look when the mist has cleared."

Millie was about to agree when an awful thought popped into her head. "But where's Jax? We still haven't found him!" She dashed on to the bridge, her heart hammering. What if there *was* something awful in the lake? What if Jax was in danger?

Jess hurried after her. Halfway across, she leaned over the wooden rail to stare into the water. "Shall we call Jax again?"

"No, don't!" Millie whispered, looking over the opposite rail. Usually the lake sparkled in the sunshine but today the water looked so deep and mysterious. "Connie must have been on the bridge when she saw the thing that scared her. Whatever it was could be really close by."

"Maybe it was an otter," said Jess.

"Although otters don't have horrible eyes."

The water beside the bridge started to ripple. Millie's hands tightened on the wooden rail. Was there something under the surface or was it just water weed?

The ripples grew deeper.

"Or perhaps it was a goose," Jess continued. "I don't like geese because of that horrible hissing noise they make."

"Jess! Look at this!" whispered Millie, watching the moving water. Whatever was causing those ripples must be right underneath the bridge.

"And swans are just as bad."

"Jess!" Millie took her friend's arm and pulled her closer. "Can you see that? Do you think something's down there?"

Jess leaned out to look just as a large shape with big black eyes floated from underneath the bridge. The beast was wrapped in water weed, making it hard to see its mouth. It had a large brownish-orange head and its glassy eyes glared at the girls spitefully.

Millie shuddered. With a head that size, goodness knows how big the rest of its body was! She wanted to run away but her legs had turned to jelly. Mist swirled over the creature, making it hard to see whether it was still staring at them.

"*What IS* that?" hissed Jess.

"Shh!" squeaked Millie. "It'll hear you!"

As if it really *had* heard, the monster spun round and glided under the bridge again.

The girls dashed to the opposite railing but the strange creature didn't reappear. Millie looked down at the wooden slats, her heart thumping. "It's right underneath us!" she whispered. "Do you think it's dangerous?"

"It doesn't look very friendly to me." Jess

leaned further over the railing. "I can't see it any more. Do you think it's dived under the water?"

"Jess, don't!" Millie tugged her friend's arm to pull her back from the edge. "What if it jumps out at you?"

Paws tapped on the bridge and Jax appeared, his coat dripping. "Jax! Thank goodness you're all right." Millie clipped his lead on quickly. "I think we should go!"

Jax barked as if he agreed. Then he galloped across the bridge, pulling Millie after him. Jess ran too and they all kept going until they reached the stable yard.

Millie stopped to catch her breath and she couldn't help staring back at the lake. Curls of mist drifted over the shore and the bridge had disappeared behind the haze. "That was so strange! Do you think it was some kind of lake monster?"

"I don't know." Jess leaned down to give Jax a rub. "I've never seen anything like it before."

An upstairs window opened and the queen's face appeared. "Amelia! Mr Larum wants you to practise your handwriting. And Jess! Mr Steen is looking for you."

Jess nudged Millie. "We'd better go back inside," she murmured. "Shame we can't have one more peek at that creature."

"Maybe we can look later!" Millie's racing heartbeat grew calmer and her eyes gleamed. "You know what? I think we've just found our next mystery!"

Chapter Three
The Legend of Spikey

Mr Steen wanted so much cleaning and polishing done that Jess didn't have much time to wonder about the creature in the lake. At five o'clock she hurried downstairs to help Cook and Connie get everything ready for the evening banquet.

A huge pot of tomato soup was bubbling on the stove and a chicken pie was baking in the oven. Connie was putting the finishing touches to Cook's dessert – a magnificent tower of jelly, meringue and strawberries, decorated with swirls of cream. Jess helped the older girl add sprinkles of chocolate to the top making the jelly tower wobble alarmingly.

Mr Steen stalked into the kitchen, his hands clasped neatly behind his back. "I've set out the gold-edged plates with the crown pattern," he told Cook Walsh. "Can you be *sure* that everything will be ready on time?"

"Of course!" Cook's face was red from leaning over the hot stove. "The pie's nearly done."

"Excellent." Mr Steen turned to Connie. "And no more talk of this ridiculous lake creature, please. I don't want our guests to get alarmed."

"I only told Queen Belinda and Cook

and the gardeners and the stable lads," protested Connie. "Oh! And the guard on the front door. Anyway I know I saw the beast, no matter what anyone says. Its eyes were terrifying – like deep black holes!"

Mr Steen gave a sniff and brushed off a speck of chocolate that Connie had dropped on his sleeve.

"Millie and I saw it too!" said Jess. "Well, we saw its head anyway. Its body was hidden under the water."

Mr Steen frowned. "There will be no talk of beasts and eyes like deep holes when we're in the banquet hall, thank you! Remember that the king and queen have guests and you must behave with dignity at all times."

Connie made a little cross sound and went back to adding chocolate sprinkles to the meringue pudding. Jess hid a smile. She didn't think anyone could have as much dignity as the butler. His clothes and hair were always perfectly neat and he never looked ruffled even for a second.

Mr Steen returned to the banquet hall

and Cook gave the soup another stir. At last everything was ready. Connie carried the large soup tureen upstairs and Jess followed her with a platter of freshly baked rolls and a dish of butter.

The hall was lit by dozens of candles. The king and queen were sitting around the great oak table with their guests. The king was telling the Duke and Duchess of Sherbourne all about the winners of last year's Peveril Palace festival.

Lady Snood was sitting beside the queen. Millie was opposite Lord Dellwort, who was smoothing his sleek moustache. Prince Edward, Millie's baby brother, had already had his tea and was upstairs being bathed by his nursemaid.

Connie began dishing out the soup and Jess followed her, offering each guest a bread roll.

"You mustn't slouch, Princess Amelia!" commanded Lady Snood. "If you sit up straight, like me, you'll look more like a lady. Can you do that?"

"Um... I'll try!" Millie sat up and immediately looked stiff and uncomfortable.

"That's better! Just be sure to lift your chin." Lady Snood stretched out her neck like a giraffe doing exercises.

Millie couldn't help giggling and had to hide her face behind her napkin.

"I hear you had a bit of a fright today, Connie," the queen said gently. "I hope it wasn't too scary."

"It was awful, Your Majesty!" replied Connie. "And to think the horrible creature I saw may have been living in the palace lake all this time."

Mr Steen, who was pouring a drink for the king, stiffened. "I don't think we should say any more about it, Connie."

"There was an olden-day legend about a monster in that lake." King James smiled broadly. "I used to enjoy hearing the tale when I was a boy."

"Yes, indeed!" The Duchess of Sherborne nodded, her grey hair shining softly in the candlelight. "A fearsome creature appeared in the lake during the reign of King Jarrod around three hundred years ago, so the story goes. It had ghastly eyes and gruesome teeth."

"And a long tail like a serpent which it thrashed around stirring up the water," added her husband, the duke. "The tale was called the Legend of Spikey. The creature was named after its sharp teeth, I think."

Millie leaned forward eagerly. "Where did it come from?"

"No one really knew," replied the duke. "Some people said it must have swum up the

River Tarry from the sea and then dragged its enormous body across to the lake one night in the darkness."

A hush settled on the banquet hall. Jess thought of the strange-looking creature they'd seen that morning. She didn't remember any sharp teeth but the beast's face had been wrapped in water weed and it had been quite misty.

"Maybe you should keep away from the lake for now," Queen Belinda said to Millie.

"Nonsense!" King James smiled. "It's just a story – that's all."

"But Jess and I saw something in the water too," Millie told him. "It didn't look very friendly and when it saw us it hid under the bridge."

"You probably just saw an otter," said the king. "There's nothing to worry about, I promise you!"

Mr Steen motioned for the girls to finish serving the food. Jess's mind was whirling as she followed Connie down the servants' corridor into the kitchen. She knew that the Legend of Spikey was just a story, but could it have been started by something that really happened long ago? Maybe what they'd seen was an ancient creature that had returned to the lake it loved.

"Come and sit down, my dears," said Cook Walsh, spooning soup into bowls and putting them on the kitchen table. She added a plate of rolls, steaming from the oven.

"Cook, have you heard an old story about a creature in the palace lake?" asked Jess.

"Ooh, yes!" Cook dipped her roll into her soup. "My mother used to tell me that tale when I was little — the Legend of Spikey. The beast was enormous, I think, and had a fondness for chicken pies."

Jess caught Mr Steen's disapproving look and didn't ask any more. As soon as dinner was over and the dishes were washed, she crept upstairs and slipped into Millie's chamber. Millie, who was already in her nightgown, was sitting on her cushioned window seat and gazing out into the darkness.

Jess sat down beside her friend. "Millie, what if the story's true? What if there *was* a lake monster and now it's returned?"

"That's just what I was thinking!" cried Millie. "Although the Duchess said the story was from three hundred years ago, so maybe it isn't *exactly* the same creature – just the same kind. Why would it want to come here though?"

"Maybe there's something here it really likes." Jess grinned. "Cook said that in the story it loved chicken pies!"

Millie laughed. "It would definitely love Cook's pies. Everything she makes is delicious!"

Jess glanced through the window. The mist from this morning had disappeared and a full moon was casting pale light across the palace garden. She leaned closer to the glass. She could just about see the lake in the darkness. Was she imagining it or were there ripples on the surface of the water? She was too far away to be sure.

"It all happened so quickly this morning," she said. "And it was so misty. Maybe the creature was a lot more ordinary than we thought."

"Don't say that!" exclaimed Millie. "It's more exciting if it's a strange monster."

Jess frowned. "We won't really know what it is unless we get another look."

Millie thought for a moment. "Maybe

we could use some food to draw it out of hiding? Monsters must need to eat!"

"Brilliant idea!" Jess's eyes gleamed. "We'll have to find somewhere safe where we can watch."

"Like up a tree!" Millie said quickly. "And we could borrow Mr Larum's telescope. He's always saying I'm welcome to use it."

"Awesome!" Jess's stomach tumbled over with excitement. "First thing tomorrow, I'll bring the food and you get the telescope, and we'll investigate the lake monster mystery together!"

Chapter Four
A Meal for a Monster

Millie got up at daybreak and tiptoed upstairs to the schoolroom. She lifted the heavy brass telescope from its metal stand and crept down the back stairs. When she went to knock on Jess's door, a loud "Psst!" made her jump.

Jess leaned round the door to the stable yard. "Hurry up!" Her eyes sparkled. "I've

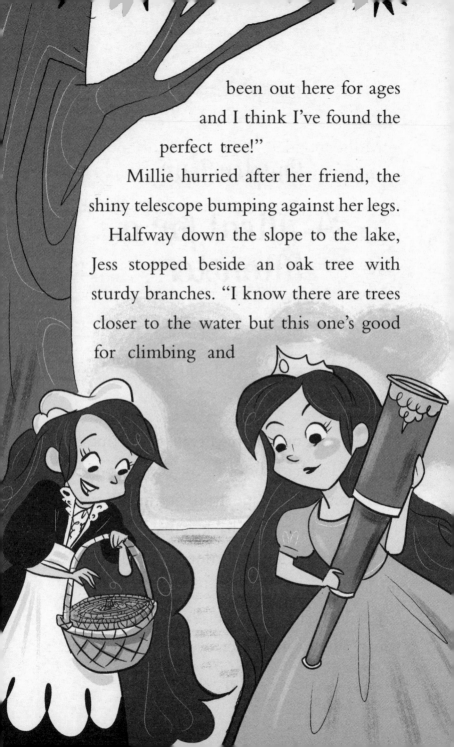

been out here for ages and I think I've found the perfect tree!"

Millie hurried after her friend, the shiny telescope bumping against her legs.

Halfway down the slope to the lake, Jess stopped beside an oak tree with sturdy branches. "I know there are trees closer to the water but this one's good for climbing and once we're up in the treetop no one will see us!"

Millie nodded. "It's great for monster-spotting!" She noticed a little wicker basket nestled in the roots of the tree. "What did you bring?"

Jess opened the lid to show her some pie wrapped in a napkin. "This is leftover chicken pie! That's what Cook said the monster in the story liked, so maybe the smell will lure it out of the water. And I brought some cherry scones in case we get hungry."

Millie propped the telescope against the tree. Then the girls took the chicken pie to the lake shore to search for a good place to put it.

"Here!" Jess pointed to a patch of reeds growing at the edge of the water. "Let's just leave it in the middle. It'll be right beside the water so the creature is sure to smell it!"

"But it might be hard to see the monster with the reeds in the way," said Millie. "I know! Why don't we break the pie into pieces and spread them out. It might trick the creature into coming out of the water."

They split the pie into four bits, placed one piece in the reeds and three more leading away from the lake. Then Millie climbed the tree, and Jess passed the telescope and the scones up to her before scrambling up too.

"We've got a great view," said Jess, between mouthfuls of scone. "Look, you can see everything!"

Millie gazed around. The sunshine made the palace's white walls gleam. A stable boy was hurrying across the yard and in the distance she could see Mr Polly, the head gardener, bending over his potato patch. The houses and church towers of

Plumchester were clustered together in the opposite direction. A horse was pulling a cart past the golden palace gates.

Lifting the telescope, Millie held it up to her eye. At once she could see every little detail – the Plumchester shopkeepers opening their blinds and the woman driving the cart dressed in a grey coat and bonnet.

She swung the telescope until it was pointing at the lake. Scanning the water, she searched for any movement especially underneath the bridge.

"Can you see anything?" Jess said eagerly.

"Nothing!" Millie passed her the telescope.

The girls watched the lake closely as the sun rose higher in the sky. A family of ducks swam over to the reeds but luckily none of them seemed interested in the pie.

"I wish the creature would hurry up."

Millie wriggled. "This branch is starting to dig into my legs."

"I've got something!" Jess blurted out. "Oh! Wait, it's just a leaf on the water."

"Let me see." Millie took the telescope, but the sound of voices made her swing it towards the palace. "My mother's coming with Mr Steen."

Jess pulled a face. "I bet he's looking for me. He probably needs more candlesticks polishing."

The girls kept quiet and still as Queen Belinda and the butler came down the slope. "Let's go to the bridge," said the queen. "From there we can plan where each stall will go. It's only two days till the festival and everything must be perfect!"

"Yes, Your Majesty." Mr Steen noticed a piece of chicken pie resting on the grass. He stooped to pick it up and stared round suspiciously before following the queen.

Millie watched him go, relieved that he hadn't looked into the tree or spotted the other pieces of pie. She scanned the lake through the telescope again and something caught her eye. The bushes on the opposite shore were squashed, as if something had come along and flattened them. She nudged Jess. "There's a big patch of squashed brambles over there. That could be a clue!"

Jess nodded seriously. "We'd better go and investigate."

Climbing down from the treetop, Millie stashed the telescope among the roots. The girls sneaked round the lake, ducking behind the boathouse and keeping out of sight as much as they could.

"Only something really heavy could have done that," said Jess, when they got to the patch of flattened brambles. "Maybe the

45

creature is bigger than we thought."

Millie spotted deep lines running across the mud on the lake shore. Her heart skipped at finding another clue. "Look at these! They're like slither marks – as if the creature's some kind of serpent!"

Jess shivered. "You mean, a gigantic water snake? I don't like the sound of that!"

"Maybe we should warn everyone." Millie glanced at her mother and the butler who were standing on the bridge.

"Mr Steen didn't believe any of it yesterday," said Jess. "I don't think he'd listen to us."

Millie knelt down beside the muddy scrape marks. She wished she'd brought a tape measure so they could work out how big the creature might be.

A loud cry broke through her thoughts. Jumping up, she saw her mother clutch Mr

Steen's arm. The queen seemed to be staring down at the water.

"Something's happened!" cried Jess. "Maybe the creature's come back."

Racing along the bank, Millie and Jess reached the bridge just as the queen began calling for the guards.

"Keep back, girls!" said Queen Belinda. "I've just seen the most horrible thing in the water."

"Is it the lake monster?" asked Millie, leaning over the rail.

"It must have been!" The queen shuddered. "We were discussing the festival and suddenly there it was – a long, slimy body twisting and turning in the water. I thought it was coming straight for us but then it sank below the surface and disappeared."

Millie leaned out a bit further, scanning the water. Excitement tickled inside her. Surely she'd get a better look at the creature this time!

"Amelia, stop that before you fall in!"

cried her mother. "Oh dear, where have the guards got to?"

At last, two guards came running to the bridge.

Jess nudged Millie. "I can't see the monster anywhere," she muttered. "But look at Mr Steen!"

The butler seemed frozen to the spot. His face had gone white and his hands were clenched around the wooden rail.

"Are you all right, Mr Steen?" asked Millie.

The butler let go of the rail and gave a squeak which he turned into a cough. "Er, yes I'm fine, thank you, Princess Amelia. But I can't have a strange creature making the lake look untidy. Something must be done about it right away!"

Chapter Five

The Trouble With Turnips

Jess stared curiously at the butler as he dabbed his forehead with a handkerchief. She'd never seen him look so pale.

The queen, who had finished describing the watery creature to the guards, noticed it too. "Jess, I think Mr Steen may need a glass of water. Could you fetch one for him?"

"Yes, Your Majesty." Jess dropped a

curtsy and ran up the hill. Her mind was buzzing. The lake monster hadn't gone for the chicken pie after all, so maybe that part of the Spikey legend was wrong. It must really like the bridge though, because it had been spotted swimming there twice. Or perhaps it was just a good place to hide.

Dashing through the back door, Jess nearly ran straight into Lady Snood coming the other way.

"Oh, sorry, Your Ladyship!" Jess sprang aside.

Lady Snood looked down her nose, saying, "Just be careful where you're going next time." Then she turned, with a swish of her velvet skirt, and went back towards the banquet hall.

Jess stared after her. What was Lady Snood doing in the servants' corridor? Guests never came this way.

"There you are at last!" Cook Walsh came out of the kitchen. "I don't know what's going on. Connie's just taken some toast and eggs to the banquet hall and come back saying most of the guests aren't there! Doesn't anyone want breakfast this morning?"

"I'm sorry I haven't been helping." Jess straightened her mob cap which had fallen over one ear. "I went outside with

Millie ... and then Queen Belinda and Mr Steen saw the lake creature ... and now Mr Steen needs a drink of water."

"Bless me! That creature is turning the whole palace upside down." Cook sighed and wiped her hands on her apron. "Well, I'll do my best with breakfast but I can't help it if the scrambled eggs go cold."

Jess fetched the glass of water and hurried back to the lake, trying not to spill it. King James and Lord Dellwort had joined the people on the bridge. Lord Dellwort was wearing a fine-looking hat with black silk around the brim.

"But what about the festival? Do you think we should cancel it?" the queen was saying to King James.

"No, we shan't let this creature ruin our special occasion," said the king. "But there must be a guard on each end of the bridge all day and all night, so if the beast gets any closer to the palace we'll know at once."

Jess exchanged looks with Millie. She knew her friend would be thinking the same – it would be harder to investigate the mystery creature with guards on the bridge all the time.

Lord Dellwort, who had been poking the water with a long stick, turned to the king and queen. "It's clear this creature – whatever it is – has made a home in this lake. I only hope it's not dangerous. I suggest the guards keep their swords ready so they can strike the beast if it comes back to the surface."

Jess's heart sank. The creature had scared her yesterday but hurting it seemed very unfair and she longed to say so.

"I'm sure there's no need for striking the creature, my Lord," said the queen, to Jess's relief. "It hasn't harmed anyone after all. Oh dear, all this excitement has made me quite hungry! Mr Steen, would you lead us into breakfast, please?"

Mr Steen bowed stiffly. "Of course, Your Majesty."

"Meet me in my chamber later," Millie whispered to Jess as she went past. "I've got a plan!"

When Jess went to Millie's chamber after breakfast, her friend was fastening the buttons on her green silk dress.

"I think we should collect as many clues about this lake creature as we can," began Millie. "There's so much to find out..."

"Like where did it come from?" put in Jess. "And if it doesn't like chicken pie then what *does* it want to eat?"

"Exactly!" Millie's cheeks turned

pink with excitement. "I want to know everything!"

"It won't be easy to get close to the bridge with the guards there," added Jess, "but the creature must have slithered into the lake from somewhere. Maybe there are more tracks in the garden."

"I've sewn paper together to make us notebooks. Now we can write everything down!" Millie proudly handed Jess a little book and a pencil. "I think we should carry

them all the time and write down clues as soon as we find them."

Jess beamed. "Mystery-solving notebooks! That's brilliant, Millie."

"Thanks!" Millie grinned.

There was a knock on the door. "Amelia," called Queen Belinda. "Mr Larum's waiting for you in the schoolroom. Don't be too long, dear."

"Bother!" whispered Millie. "Now I'll be stuck inside for ages and I really wanted to start looking for clues."

"I can start searching," Jess told her. "If I wear one of your dresses then Mr Steen won't stop me and give me lots of chores."

"Good idea!" Millie dashed over to her wardrobe and took out a pale blue dress.

Jess changed quickly and hid her maid uniform in the bottom of the cupboard.

"Now you just need a tiara." Millie took

off her sparkling silver crown and put it on Jess's head.

"Thanks, Double Trouble!" Jess grinned and the girls linked their little fingers. "I just hope no one notices that you're wearing two different dresses all at the same time!"

Jess slipped out through the courtyard without anyone stopping her. She'd hidden the little notebook and pencil inside her sleeve – it was best no one saw it and started asking questions. Grey clouds had drifted across the sky, cutting out the sunshine.

She went to the rose garden first but there was nothing out of place. Moving on, she looked around the croquet lawn before checking every passageway of the maze. This part of the palace garden was a long way from the lake, but Jess had decided she must look everywhere. Her mother and father, who owned a dressmaking shop in Plumchester, had always told her that if a task was important she should do it carefully.

Sitting down on the croquet lawn to catch her breath, she started writing in her mystery-solving notebook.

Lake creature, she wrote and underlined it carefully. Then she added underneath, *Is it Spikey from the famous legend?*

Then she tried to draw the monster's head. It was hard to get the picture just right. It had been so misty yesterday and the creature hadn't stayed still for very long.

Lastly she wrote: *It didn't eat the chicken pie.*

Tucking the notebook away, she walked through the orchard and stopped by the vegetable patch where Mr Polly was raking the earth in a fierce manner. He didn't even look up as she came along.

"Hello, Mr Polly," called Jess. "Is everything all right?"

Mr Polly stopped and leaned on his rake. "No, I'm afraid it's not, Princess Amelia! Some scoundrel has ruined my turnips – ripped them right out of the ground! They've spoiled my potato plants too. It's an absolute disgrace!"

Jess suddenly realized that where Mr Polly was standing there used to be a row of purple-topped turnips. Now it was just bare earth. Was this something to do with the lake monster?

She stepped closer. Mr Polly had raked most of the soil but in one corner there were deep scrape marks. Jess caught her breath. Those looked just like the slithery tracks that Millie had spotted on the lake shore. Her heart raced. "When were the turnips stolen?"

Mr Polly shook his head. "Sometime last night. I found the place in a mess when I got up this morning." He started raking again. "It'll take weeks to grow new plants. What a shame!"

"Why don't I fetch you a cup of hot chocolate from the kitchen," said Jess, hurrying away. She felt sorry for poor Mr

Polly but at least she finally had a proper clue!

Now she understood why the creature from the lake hadn't eaten the chicken pie. It was already full after eating all those vegetables!

Chapter Six
Collecting the Clues

Millie stared out of the schoolroom window, wondering whether Jess had found any clues.

Mr Larum was reading to her from a book about Peveril Palace in the olden days. At last he broke off and straightened his dark-rimmed glasses. "Shall we stop for today, Princess Amelia? I can see you're far too excited about the festival to think about anything else."

"Yes, please." Millie smiled. She didn't tell him she was more excited about the lake monster than the festival. Mr Larum might think it wasn't the sort of thing a princess should be excited about. She helped him wipe the chalkboard clean before rushing downstairs.

Hurrying out of the back door, Millie scanned the stable yard. She knew Jess must be out here somewhere. They were sure to run into each other and then they could compare clues. She tucked the mystery-solving notebook and pencil inside her sleeve. There was no time to lose!

Crossing the stable yard, she stopped at the top of the slope. The wind blew strongly, rippling the surface of the lake. Two guards were standing to attention on opposite ends of the bridge. Millie knew she needed a reason to get past them. She needed an excuse for going to the lake shore. But what could it be?

An idea popped into her head. Two weeks ago she'd lost a white handkerchief while taking Jax for a walk. She could search for that and at the same time look for clues! Skipping down the slope, she explained to the guards all about her missing hanky.

"I wish I could help you look, Princess Amelia," said the chief guard, a man with red cheeks and a bushy moustache. "But my orders are very clear. I must stay here on the bridge unless the water monster appears."

"Oh, don't worry! I can search for it by myself," said Millie, hurrying on.

"Be careful, Your Highness," called the guard. "Don't go too near the shore."

Millie waved to show she'd heard him. She knew she should be sensible, but at the same time looking for the monster made her stomach flip over with excitement. Imagine if it suddenly popped up from below! Anyway the creature hadn't hurt anyone and seemed to want to hide most of the time, so she felt quite safe.

Hurrying round the shore, Millie looked for muddy tracks and other monster signs. When she reached the squashed brambles, she spotted water weed stretched along the bank as if it had fallen off the creature's body when it came out of the water.

Perching on a rock, she took out her notebook and pencil and scribbled down what she'd found. Then she tried to draw the monster – his black eyes and blotchy face. It was harder than she expected. She frowned. Maybe Jess could remember the monster's face a bit better.

Feeling hungry, she hurried back towards the kitchen hoping Cook might give her a freshly baked roll. The sun came out again and the Duke and Duchess of Sherborne were crossing the stable yard, arm in arm.

"Morning, my dear," said the duke. "Have you seen the lake creature today?"

"I can't see it anywhere," said Millie. "Maybe it likes to hide."

"Maybe." The duchess studied her with wise grey eyes. "But I'd advise you to be careful. Sometimes when you search for things you can end up finding more than you expected."

Millie was about to ask what she meant, but just then Jess burst out of the back door wearing Millie's pale blue dress.

"Um, well, I must go," gabbled Millie, hoping that the duke and duchess wouldn't turn round and see another princess who looked like her twin.

Jess spun round and dashed back inside.

Millie said goodbye to the duke and duchess before going after her friend. She caught up with Jess in the kitchen where Cook Walsh was taking a large cake out of the oven.

"That was close!" gasped Jess. "It was lucky they didn't see me."

"Goodness me, you're princess twins!" chuckled Cook Walsh, setting the cake on the table. "One of you had better put a maid's dress on before Mr Steen walks in."

"I will!" said Millie eagerly. "Then can I help you decorate that cake?"

Cook smiled. "Of course you can. I'm making raspberry icing for this one."

Millie changed her clothes in Jess's chamber and returned in her friend's spare maid uniform and mob cap. Then, while Cook was mixing the icing, she and Jess swapped notebooks and studied each other's clues.

"The lake monster likes vegetables? I can't believe it!" cried Millie, when she read Jess's notes.

"The vegetable garden was in such a mess," Jess told her. "Most of the turnips were gone and quite a few potatoes too. Mr Polly was really upset."

"But at least we know the creature's not hungry," said Millie.

Jess held her picture of the monster next to Millie's drawing. "You made its head a different shape and you've drawn its eyes bigger too."

"I know!" Millie stared at the two pictures. "It was hard to remember how it looked. We only saw the creature for a minute and it was very misty." She wrinkled her forehead. "It does make me wonder..."

"About what?"

"My mother said the monster's body was

long and slimy and that made me think of a serpent. But its head didn't look like a serpent's at all!"

"Maybe he's a mixed-up monster with the head of one thing and the body of another." Jess shrugged.

"Poor Spikey!" Millie shook her head. "He must be the strangest-looking monster that's ever come to Plumchester."

Millie had to change back into her royal clothes and swap tiaras with Jess before hurrying down to dinner that evening. The table in the banquet hall was laid out ready, with every spoon polished and every crystal glass gleaming. Mr Steen was circling the table and handing out snowy-white napkins.

Millie glanced nervously at Lady Snood. She hoped her ladyship wouldn't start giving her instructions on how to sit this time.

King James was telling Lord Dellwort all about the musicians that would play at the festival but the talk soon turned back to the lake monster once again.

"Seeing that creature moving in the water gave me quite a scare." Queen Belinda smoothed her velvet gown. She was wearing the Sky Sapphire necklace and the pretty blue gem glowed in the candlelight.

"At least the creature's done no harm," said the Duchess of Sherborne. "The beast in the Spikey legend ate all the palace chickens!"

"How terrible!" cried Lady Snood. "That behaviour is not respectable, even for a monster."

"No one knows if it really happened," replied the duchess. "That's just how the story goes."

"I think the creature likes vegetables not

chickens," Millie told them. "It's stolen some vegetables from the garden."

No one took any notice of this and Millie wriggled crossly. She and Jess had spent ages collecting clues. Well, she wasn't going to share anything else if the grown-ups wouldn't listen!

"Perhaps it would be a good idea to raise the alarm if the creature is spotted again. All you need to do is give the guards something that makes a noise – a bell maybe." Lord Dellwort smoothed his moustache. "Then all the palace guards can join the ones on the bridge to fight danger."

"I think that would work well," said Queen Belinda.

"Indeed!" King James looked thoughtful. "In fact, if they use a horn and a drum the noise will be even louder. I shall organize it immediately."

Everyone joined in, saying what a good idea it was. Only Lady Snood stayed quiet. Millie noticed that she kept shooting glances at the queen's sapphire necklace.

"That's settled then," said King James. "The guards will sound a warning as soon as they see the creature."

"And I think it would be best if no one went near the lake unless they're with a guard," added Queen Belinda. "Safety is the most important thing."

Millie's heart sank. That meant that she and Jess wouldn't be able to get close to the water. So how could they *ever* find out more about the lake creature?

Chapter Seven

The Shadow on the Wall

"I think we should go outside tonight and look for Spikey." Jess hugged her knees. She was sitting on the window seat in Millie's chamber in her dressing gown. Cook Walsh had let her bring two mugs of hot chocolate upstairs and some cookies that were left over from lunch.

Outside the window, a cluster of stars winked in the night sky.

"Do you think we really should?" Millie sipped her hot chocolate. "We'll be in trouble if the guards see us. My mother said no one should go down to the lake by themselves."

"Staying hidden will be easier in the dark," Jess pointed out. "And now we know how much the monster loves vegetables we can take it some."

"But won't it be harder to see it in the dark?" said Millie, doubtfully.

"We have to try!" said Jess. "What if the guards see the monster first and strike it with their swords like Lord Dellwort said? They could hurt the poor thing!" She gazed at her friend pleadingly. Millie sometimes took longer to decide about things but she loved animals so Jess was sure she'd agree.

"You're right!" said Millie at last. "Spikey may need our help."

"Let's go now!" said Jess, eagerly. "Cook will be in her chamber and the servants' corridor will be empty. No one will see us."

Jax, who had gone to sleep on the end of Millie's bed, woke up and wagged his tail.

"I'm sorry, Jax." Millie went over and stroked him. "We can't take you with us this time."

Jax barked softly and closed his eyes again.

The girls swapped their dressing gowns for black cloaks that would help them stay hidden in the dark. Tiptoeing down the back stairs, they lit a lantern in the kitchen before gathering turnips, potatoes and carrots from the pantry.

"This will be enough." Millie loaded the vegetables into a basket. "Let's go!"

When they stepped out into the stable

yard, Jess lifted the lantern shakily. Her heart was thumping. She knew she had to be ready to blow out the lantern if anyone came along. The wind whistled round the palace towers and a soft hooting came from somewhere in the dark sky.

"It's spooky out here," whispered Millie.

"You won't go back, will you?" said Jess. "I'm not sure I want to do this on my own."

Millie took Jess's hand. "Course I won't!"

They ran across the yard and hid behind the stable wall on the other side. Jess took some deep breaths, hoping her stomach would stop tumbling over and over. At least here they were out of sight of the palace windows.

She scanned the darkness. The lake was a patch of deep black at the bottom of the hill. Two little dots of light moved on the bridge in the middle.

"Those lights must be the guards and if we can see their lanterns, they might see ours!" hissed Millie.

Jess blew out the lantern, leaving them in darkness. Luckily, as they went gingerly down the slope, a full moon drifted out from behind a cloud and lit the way.

"I think we should go back to where we found those tracks," whispered Jess. "Then, if we throw the vegetables into the water, Spikey might come to eat them."

They crept along the lake shore, searching for the place with the creature's tracks. The moon dipped behind a cloud, plunging them back into darkness. Jess tripped over a tree root and Millie tore her cloak on a bramble, but at last they found the large scrape marks in the mud.

Jess took a turnip from the basket, her hand shaking with excitement. She flung the vegetable at the water. It landed with a splash before bobbing up and down.

"I didn't know it would float," said Millie.

"I didn't know that either. I wonder if this will too." Jess threw a potato in but it sank instantly.

"Let's stick to the turnips," said Millie, throwing a second one at the water. "Then the lake monster will come to the surface to eat them. I wonder if it'll nibble them or just swallow them with one big gulp!"

"I bet it gulps them! I wonder—" Jess broke off. What was that rustling in the bushes?

A shape burst from the undergrowth and leapt into the lake, making an enormous splash. Water splattered over Millie and Jess, drenching their cloaks.

Millie gave a shriek, pointing to the dark shape. "It's here! It's the monster!"

"Shh! The guards will hear you!" Jess's

heart hammered as she stared at the thing in the water. It was so dark. She wished she hadn't put out the lantern. The monster seemed to be paddling around close to the shore. Was it busy eating the turnips?

Suddenly, the monster sprang on to the bank beside them, before shaking the water off its coat. It gave a soft bark.

"Jax!" cried Millie. "Oh, you scared me!"

"What are you doing here, Jax?" Jess hugged the soggy dog. "You were meant to stay inside."

Millie giggled. "We must have left the back door open a little and Jax decided he didn't like us having an adventure without him!"

Jess glanced up. The guards' lanterns were moving closer. "They're coming!" She nudged Millie. "We have to go."

Jess held on to Jax as they crept along the shore. Ducking behind the boathouse, she stopped to look back. The guards' lanterns had stopped moving too.

"Maybe they're looking at the turnips we threw in," whispered Millie. "Do you think they saw us?"

"I don't think they were close enough to see it was us." Jess put down the lantern to shake a stone out of her shoe. Jax broke away, bounding towards the front of the boathouse.

"Jax, come back!" hissed Millie, running after him.

Jess quickly got her shoe back on and chased after them. The moon floated out from behind a cloud just as she rounded the corner of the wooden building. A tall, dark shadow stretched up the boathouse wall.

It was shaped like a person.

Icy prickles ran down Jess's neck. Was someone standing there? The shadow wasn't Millie's. She was crouching down beside Jax, rubbing his coat and talking softly into his ear. It couldn't be one of the guards – they were still far away.

"Millie?" croaked Jess, her eyes fixed on the patch of darkness.

The shadow moved. A figure crashed through the bushes and disappeared in the direction of the stables.

"What was that?" Millie's eyes widened. "Someone else was here!"

"I didn't see them properly!" Jess's mind

whirled. "They ran away pretty fast." She noticed the door to the boathouse was open slightly. Pushing her way in, she looked around in astonishment.

Piles of earth-smeared vegetables lay across the wooden floor next to a heap of sacks and string. Jax pattered inside, sniffing at the mound of turnips and potatoes.

"What are these doing here? Do you think they came from the vegetable garden?" Millie went pale. "Maybe this is the monster's lair!"

"But monsters can't open doors," Jess pointed out. "Somebody must have carried the vegetables here – and they must be the same person that messed up Mr Polly's garden."

"They're feeding the lake monster in secret!" said Millie. "But *why*?"

"And what are the sacks and the string

for?" Jess's heart skipped. "This mystery is bigger than I thought and this is our best clue yet!"

Chapter Eight

Mr Steen Gets Flustered

The guards' lanterns were drawing closer, so Millie and Jess left the boathouse and hurried up the hill in the dark. Every rustle in the bushes made Millie nervous. Where was the shadowy figure? Was he waiting behind a tree?

A shiver ran down her back and she sped up, the basket of vegetables bumping against her legs as she ran. Jax reached the back door first and pawed at the handle, whining. Jess swung the door open and they all bundled inside.

Millie hurried to the pantry to put back the vegetables. "Whoever left those turnips in the boathouse must know more about the monster than we do," she said breathlessly. "Maybe they've known what kind of creature it is all along!"

Jess's eyes gleamed. "So if we find out who it is, we'll find out everything about the monster."

"Exactly!" said Millie.

There were footsteps in the passage. "Who's in here?" called Cook Walsh.

"It's only me and Jess." Millie peeked round the pantry door. "Sorry, Cook! We're just going to bed, I promise."

"I should think so too – wandering round in the middle of the night! It's ridiculous!

There was someone on the stairs just now as well. It's not right to wake me up." Cook went away, grumbling.

"Let's talk about it in the morning," Millie whispered to Jess and she led Jax up the stairs to her chamber.

Pulling off her cloak, Millie peered out of her window. The dots of light from the guards' lanterns were still moving in the dark, but the wind had dropped and the lake was still.

Millie climbed into bed and closed her eyes. Strange, black-eyed monsters with turnip legs went swimming through her dreams.

At breakfast the next morning, Millie studied everyone carefully to see who was looking suspicious. She was so busy staring round the table that she nearly poured apple

juice on Mr Steen, who was trying to tidy
the napkins.

Jess, who was bringing in a tray of boiled eggs, muttered in her ear, "Lady Snood looks tired. Maybe she was the one by the lake last night."

Lady Snood tapped crossly on the top of her egg with her spoon. She certainly seemed in a bad temper but Millie couldn't picture her ladyship plodding along the muddy lake shore in the dark.

Queen Belinda handed Prince Edward to his nursemaid and beamed at everyone. "It's so exciting to think that the festival begins tomorrow! Mr Steen and I are going to spend today getting everything ready. Cloth tents will be put up on the croquet lawn as that's furthest away from the lake and any ... er ... interruptions."

"The guards heard a noise around midnight last night," added King James. "But when they searched the spot nothing was there. So perhaps the lake creature has gone."

Millie stared at her napkin. She was sure the noise had been her and Jess.

Lord Dellwort raised his eyebrows doubtfully. "Is the creature *really* likely to have gone?"

Lady Snood shuddered. "Perhaps it's waiting till the festival begins. Then it will be able to terrify more people!"

The queen's smile vanished. "Oh, I hope not! Usually everyone in Plumchester comes to the festival. It's always been a very happy day."

"And I'm sure it will be this time too," said the duchess with a kindly smile. "We're looking forward to it."

"Do let us know if you want any help," added the duke.

"Thank you, I will! Mr Steen?" Queen Belinda looked round for the royal butler.

"Mr Steen, are you there? I'm ready to begin our preparations."

Mr Steen appeared in the doorway, his face pale. "I'm sorry, Your Majesty! I must speak to Jess and Connie before we begin."

"Very well!" The queen smiled. "Find me as soon as you're ready."

"Yes, Your Majesty." The butler bowed jerkily.

Jess put down her boiled eggs and followed Mr Steen into the hallway. Connie, who had just come in with a jug of apple juice, went too. Millie quickly ate one more mouthful of toast and slipped out of the banquet hall. She had a feeling something was wrong.

"What have you done with the key to the Royal Jewel Cabinet?" the butler was asking Jess and Connie. "Did you lose it somewhere?"

"No," said Jess, surprised. "Isn't it in the State Room with all the other keys?"

"I haven't got it." Connie sniffed and folded her arms.

Mr Steen frowned at the maids. "I'm sure I left it in the right place when I locked everything up last night. Did you take it when you were cleaning this morning?"

"No, I haven't been into the State Room yet," said Connie.

"Well, the king and queen certainly don't have it." Mr Steen twisted his hands together. "Such a terrible week! First a monster in the lake and now this! Every treasure in the palace is kept in that cabinet."

Millie dashed into the State Room. Going to the wooden desk, she lifted the lid and hunted inside. There were lots of keys – large ones, tiny ones and rusty ones – but the shiny silver key that unlocked the jewel cabinet wasn't there. "He's right – it's gone!" she told Jess, who had followed her.

Jess rattled the door to the cabinet. "But this is still locked and it doesn't look like anything is missing."

Millie scanned the shelves. Everything was there – the shiny goblets, the sparkling crowns and the beautiful Sky Sapphire necklace.

Mr Steen, who had been questioning the guard at the door, marched in with a face like a storm cloud and stared into the cabinet. Millie could almost see him ticking off every single tiara, bracelet and ring inside his head. "Mr Steen?" she said timidly. "We could help you look for the key if you want?"

The butler turned stiffly and arched one eyebrow. "That is very kind, Princess Amelia, but I'm sure you have more important royal duties. Jess, don't forget to clear up the breakfast plates." He swept from the room and called a guard over, saying, "Guard this door! *No one* is allowed in here except me or the king and queen."

"Yes, sir," replied the guard.

Millie and Jess went back to the banquet hall to find it empty. Taking the last slice of lemon loaf, Millie cut it in two and gave half to Jess. She wandered to the front of the hall and sat down on the queen's red velvet throne, thinking hard while she ate. Jess glanced round before sitting beside her on the king's throne.

Millie brushed the crumbs off her skirt. "First there's a creature in the lake and now there's a missing key. I wish it all made more sense!"

"Maybe Mr Steen lost the key himself and he just doesn't want to admit it," said Jess.

Millie sprang to her feet and started walking up and down. "He's never lost anything before!"

"But he's been acting funny ever since he saw the monster." Jess's eyes widened. "Do you think it was him by the boathouse last night?"

"I don't think so! Why would he run away when we came along?"

Jess's forehead wrinkled. "Well, someone was down there in the dark..."

"You're right!" Millie took Jess's hand and pulled her up. "And I bet whoever it was will try to sneak back there to finish what they were doing. If we watch the place we can discover exactly who it is!"

Chapter Nine
Sacks and String

Jess and Millie took the breakfast plates to the kitchen before slipping out past the stables. The lake glittered at the bottom of the hill. A family of ducks were paddling by the water reeds and two bored-looking guards stood on the bridge with a drum and a horn by their feet.

The girls hid between two patches of brambles, making sure they had a good view of the boathouse.

"What if someone goes inside?" said Jess. "We won't be able to see what they're doing."

"We could use the telescope again. That way we'll see through the window without needing to get close. I'll go and get it!" Millie squeezed out of the brambles and hurried away.

Jess waited. She wriggled to free herself from a thorny branch that was pressing against her arm. How long would Millie be? Had she found the telescope yet?

A few minutes went by. Jess tried to think of all the clues they'd found so far. The one that really puzzled her was the missing key to the Royal Jewel Cabinet. Why would someone take that key? There was always a guard standing at the front door so no one could sneak in and open the cabinet anyway.

Two figures moved among the trees by the boathouse. The Duke and Duchess of Sherborne walked arm in arm round the corner of the little wooden building and stopped to peer through its dusty window.

Jess held her breath. Had the duke and duchess been secretly feeding the lake creature all along?

Untangling herself from the brambles, Jess crept down the slope towards them. The duke and duchess opened the boathouse door and stepped inside.

Jess glanced back. Where was Millie? She was missing this important clue!

One of the guards on the bridge raised his arm and pointed at her. He'd seen her sneaking down the hill! Jess's heart sank. Straightening her apron, she carried on walking. She had to know what the duke and duchess were up to.

The guards began to shout.

Jess looked back and her heart flipped over. The men weren't pointing at her at all. Something dark and bumpy was sliding across the lake. It must be Spikey! The creature moved towards the bridge, the water churning round its body.

Jess ran to the water's edge, excitement

fizzing inside her. The creature looked so lumpy! She'd expected its body to be more like a gigantic water snake – all long and smooth. Its head looked different from the way she remembered too.

For a moment, the monster sank below the surface. Then it reappeared a little further on. Its deep black eyes stared forward without blinking.

The guards stood as if they were frozen.

"Blow the horn!" shouted Jess. "Sound the alarm!"

The men jumped into action. One picked up the horn and the other dashed to get the drum. Then they banged and blew their instruments until the noise echoed across the lake.

The monster slowed down beside the reeds and something broke off its side before floating away on the rippling water.

The first guard went on pounding the drum. The other blew the horn until his cheeks turned red and he stopped to take a gasping breath. Two grooms ran down the hill from the stables. A moment later, Mr Polly hurried after them, his wellies caked with mud and a pitchfork in his hand.

"Over here!" called the guard with the drum, and the men hurried towards the water reeds where the monster was lurking.

A minute later, the king, the queen and Lady Snood rushed down the slope and everyone started pointing and talking at once. More guards ran from the direction of the palace, their swords held ready.

Cook Walsh appeared with a rolling pin and Connie ran up with a mop in her hand. Mr Steen hovered at the back of the crowd, twisting his long fingers together.

Millie came flying past them all. "Jess!" she gasped. "You found the monster!"

"I guess so." Jess stared at the water. The piece that had fallen off the monster looked strangely familiar.

"Stand back, everyone!" called King James. "This creature could be very dangerous."

Mr Steen tutted in disapproval. "Jess, what are *you* doing here? Didn't I find you enough sweeping to do?"

"Um..." Jess's eyes were fixed on the water.

Why was the creature waiting by the reeds? Why wasn't it swimming away from this noisy crowd of people? Maybe something was wrong with it.

Another lump broke off its body and bobbed away on the water. It was purplish-brown with a smooth round shape.

"It's breaking apart!" said Millie, astonished.

Jess edged out till the water lapped at her shoes. The closer she got the more odd things she noticed. The creature's skin was bumpy like a sack. Pieces of string were wound across its body and its black eyes were dull.

The purple-brown lump floated over to the bank and Jess picked it out of the water. "It's a turnip!" she cried. "The monster's not real!"

Millie's mouth dropped open.

"Be careful there, Princess Amelia and Miss Jess!" Mr Polly waded into the shallows in his wellies. Lifting his pitchfork, he caught the middle of the monster with its prongs.

Lady Snood gave a muffled shriek and covered her eyes with her handkerchief.

A cluster of turnips escaped from the monster's skin and drifted away. A duck paddled over to peck at one of the vegetables before deciding it wasn't tasty after all. Mr Polly scooped up the rest of the creature with his pitchfork, lifted it out of the water and tipped the dripping mass on to the grass. The torn sack bulged with more turnips. The black eyes – just circles of black material – sat crookedly on top.

"It's all sacking and string!" cried the queen. "But ... I was sure I'd seen a monster."

The king chuckled. "Someone's been playing a joke on us all! A monster indeed! I never really believed it."

"The turnips must have kept the whole thing afloat." Millie's eyes were wide. "Remember, Jess! They were the vegetable that didn't sink."

"The sacking will have weighed it down to make it disappear under the water a lot of the time," said Mr Polly. "What a waste of good turnips."

"More like the legend of veggie than the legend of Spikey!" Lord Dellwort straightened his hat and grinned.

"Goodness me, how odd!" said the

duchess, arriving arm in arm with the duke. "We've just been inside the boathouse and there are quite a lot of turnips in there too."

"Well, whoever it was can own up now. You had us all fooled!" The king smiled. "Come on, who was it?"

Everyone looked around. Lady Snood glared at Mr Polly. Cook Walsh stared at Lady Snood. The queen frowned worriedly and silence settled on the group.

Jess felt a wriggling in her stomach. "Something's wrong," she whispered to Millie. "Why would someone spend ages making a pretend monster? And why aren't they owning up?"

"It must have been someone here," murmured Millie. "Everyone in the whole palace has come."

Jess's strange wriggly feeling grew stronger. "Maybe that's what the monster-maker wants — for everyone to leave the palace at once — the guards, the guests, everybody!"

Millie frowned. "You mean . . . they want the palace to be empty?"

Suddenly the clues slotted together like a jigsaw in Jess's head — the pretend monster and the missing key. "Maybe they want to do something bad while no one's around — like open the Royal Jewel Cabinet!"

"Then we haven't got much time!" gasped Millie.

The girls broke through the crowd and raced up the hill to the palace at top speed.

Chapter Ten
The Empty Palace

Millie ran as fast as she could and managed to keep up with Jess all the way to the front entrance. With no guard to stop them they dashed straight inside.

The empty silence of the palace made Millie's skin prickle. Her footsteps sounded so loud on the tiled floor. She jumped as the clock tinged and the cuckoo popped out to call the time.

"There's no guard here either." Jess dashed

into the State Room. "It's too late — the cabinet's open!"

Millie's heart sank as she saw the missing silver key stuck in the cabinet door. Pulling the door wide, she scanned the shelves full of shiny goblets and glittering crowns. "Everything's still here," she breathed. "No, wait! I think the Sky Sapphire's gone."

"You're right — it's not here," said Jess.

Millie swallowed. "Mother will be so sad. Father gave her that necklace on their wedding day."

"The king's always saying the Sky Sapphire's the most valuable jewel in the kingdom," sighed Jess. "No wonder they took it."

"I wish they'd taken anything except that! But ... oh!" Millie's eyes grew big and round. "I think I know who stole it! Lady Snood couldn't take her eyes off the sapphire from the first minute she saw it."

"And I saw her sneaking down the servants' corridor when I fetched water for Mr Steen that time!" Jess frowned and then shook her head. "But she was at the lake just now with everyone else so how could she have stolen the jewel?"

Footsteps sounded in the entrance hall and King James marched into the room with Mr Steen trailing behind him.

"Amelia, what's going on?" boomed the king. "Steen keeps going on about a missing key, and you and Jess ran off just now like deer being chased by a lion."

Millie explained that the Sky Sapphire was gone and how they thought it was all mixed up with the pretend lake monster. The guards returned in the middle of it all and everyone crowded into the State Room to gaze at the jewel cabinet.

The king's eyebrows lowered. "You

mean the lake creature was made by some scoundrel to distract us? I've never heard of anything so wicked!"

"Don't worry, Your Majesty!" the chief guard told him. "We'll find the queen's sapphire if we have to search every corner of Peveril Palace. We'll ask each person to turn out their pockets too." He sent a man to stand at the bottom of the grand staircase to keep everyone away while the guards began searching the upper floors.

"I don't know who would do something like this," said Queen Belinda sadly. "That necklace meant so much to me."

"I'm sure the guards will find it," said the Duke of Sherborne.

"Perhaps a nice cup of tea would help," added the duchess. "Why don't we all go into the parlour and sit down while the guards finish their search."

"I'll bring tea for everyone," said Jess, quickly. "And some of Cook's butterfly cakes."

Millie and Jess went to the kitchen and Jess set the copper kettle on the stove while Millie put butterfly cakes on a china plate. Her mind was spinning. Had the lake monster been a fake all along? When they'd seen it from the bridge that first time it had looked very different from the lumpy sack monster.

Millie carried the plate of cakes to the door. There was a rustle of skirts at the end of the passage and a figure disappeared up the back stairs. "Jess!" hissed Millie. "Lady Snood's just gone up the servants' stairs. She must be trying to avoid the guards!"

Jess ran out. "Do you think she's hiding the Sky Sapphire? Are you sure it was her?"

"I think so!" Millie put down the plate

and dashed to the stairs with Jess behind her. When they got to the top, they saw Lady Snood's door swing closed.

Jess pulled Millie back as a guard came out of Lord Dellwort's room. When he was gone, they slipped over to her ladyship's door and listened closely. Muffled thuds came from inside. Millie and Jess exchanged looks.

"What are we going to say?" whispered Millie.

"I don't know! Let's just make it up as we go." Jess knocked smartly and went in.

Lady Snood went pink when she saw them and put something behind her back. "What's this?" she snapped. "I didn't expect to be disturbed."

"I'm sorry, Your Ladyship." Jess dropped a curtsy. "I just wondered if you'd like your chamber swept."

Millie tried to see what Lady Snood was hiding but her ladyship kept her arm firmly behind her back.

"No, I don't want my room cleaned just now." Lady Snood looked down her long nose. "Please go and shut the door behind you."

"Perhaps we could bring you a cup of tea and a butterfly cake?" Millie edged closer.

"No, thank you! I'm not thirsty—" Lady Snood dropped something and a bunched-up piece of white material fell to the floor. "Oh bother! Now see what you made me do."

The material unrolled as her ladyship picked it up again. It was a pair of long, white bloomers with extra lace around the legs of the knickers.

"Oh!" Millie's eyes went as round as teacups. "Well . . . um . . . we really shouldn't disturb you any more."

"Now you're here you may as well help," snapped Lady Snood, whipping more frilly underwear out of the drawer. "I *really* can't have those guards rummaging through my undergarments when they search my room. I need somewhere to put them."

Millie bit her lip as she tried not to giggle. "We'll fetch a basket and keep your garments in the laundry room," she told Lady Snood.

The girls fetched the basket and, once Lady Snood had stuffed her underwear inside, Millie laid a thick cloak over the top. They took the basket downstairs and stored it safely in the laundry room.

"If Lady Snood was really the thief she would have been hiding the jewel, not her underwear," said Millie as they closed the laundry door. "I think we were wrong about her."

"Who could it be then?" asked Jess.

"I wish I knew! We can't let them get away with it." Millie glanced out of the window. Dark clouds hung low over the lake. Yesterday they had been hunting for the monster and everything had seemed strange and exciting, but the creature wasn't real and her mother's sapphire necklace was gone.

"Whoever took the jewel must have been waiting for the right moment," said Jess.

"I was thinking that too!" Millie rubbed her aching forehead. "The thief knew that it was safe to slip into the State Room once the guards sounded the alarm. Whoever it was took the sapphire and then came to the lake to join everyone else."

"Which means they must have been one of the last people to get there," added Jess. "So it wasn't the Duke and Duchess of Sherborne. I saw them go into the boathouse."

Millie's heart skipped a beat. "I know who arrived last! He was the one that suggested sounding the alarm too. He planned the whole thing!"

"Who?" Jess stared. "Millie, who is it?"

Millie spun round and started running. "He's probably still got the Sky Sapphire," she called back. "I'm going to catch him before he gets away!"

Chapter Eleven
The Hidden Jewel

Jess and Millie stopped in the parlour doorway, trying to catch their breath. The king, the queen, Lord Dellwort, Lady Snood and the duke and duchess were sitting near the fireplace. Connie was pouring cups of tea for them all. "It's all right," she said looking pointedly at Jess. "I finished making the tea for you."

"Thanks, Connie." Jess scanned the guests. Who was Millie talking about?

She tried to picture everyone by the lake that morning. Who had been the last to get there? Not the guards or Mr Polly or Connie and certainly not the Duke and Duchess of Sherborne. Suddenly, she noticed Lord Dellwort smirking as he twirled his moustache.

She nudged Millie, muttering, "Do you think it's him?"

"I'm sure it is!" Millie whispered fiercely. "See how smug he looks."

The chief guard entered, bowing to the king and queen. "Sorry for the interruption, Your Majesties. We're searching for the sapphire and we're asking everyone in the palace to turn out their pockets."

The king began to wave him away. "There's no need for our guests to do that."

"It's quite all right!" The Duke of Sherborne showed the guard his empty pockets. Then each guest did the same. The duchess even opened her little golden purse which was full of face powder and perfume.

Jess held her breath when it was Lord Dellwort's turn but he smiled broadly and showed everyone his empty pockets. The girls exchanged looks. Where was the Sky Sapphire?

"It's a shame that such a precious jewel has gone missing." Lord Dellwort sat down and straightened his hat. "Do you think I could have some more tea?"

Millie glared at him. "I think you know EXACTLY where the Sky Sapphire is because you took it!"

"Amelia!" gasped Queen Belinda. "Apologize to his lordship."

"But, Mother – I'm sure that he planned the whole thing!" cried Millie. "He went to the jewel cabinet when everyone else ran down to the lake."

"That's enough!" The queen went pink. "We do not say things like that to our guests. Now apologize at once or you won't be allowed to go to the festival tomorrow."

Jess stepped forward before Millie could reply. She had been gazing at Lord Dellwort's hat with its black silk band around the brim. Why was he wearing it? He wasn't outdoors and it wasn't cold in the parlour.

Maybe there was another reason for keeping it on. Someone as sneaky as Lord Dellwort was much too clever to hide the jewel in his pocket.

"Excuse me, sir," she said, curtsying. "Shall I take your hat for you?"

Lord Dellwort held the hat to his head. "No, thank you. I prefer to wear it."

Jess nudged Millie.

"Oh, hat!" Millie's eyebrows rose. "Um … yes! I'm so sorry about what I said just now, Your Lordship. I don't know why I was so silly. Let me pour you that cup of tea you asked for." She went to Lord Dellwort, offering to take his teacup.

While he was looking at Millie, Jess sneaked up behind him. With a sudden sweep of her arm, she knocked his hat to the floor.

"JESS!" cried Queen Belinda, then she stopped.

The hat lay upturned on the floor. Inside was a necklace with a beautiful sky blue jewel shaped like a teardrop. Millie picked up the delicate gold chain and the sapphire spun gently, glistening in the light.

"It was you all along!" King James looked stunned.

"Nonsense! This is just a mistake," Lord Dellwort blustered. "I don't know how that necklace got there."

"Yes, you do!" Jess told him. "First, you stole the key to the jewel cabinet – you probably took it out of Mr Steen's pocket. Then all you had to do was find a way to get to the cabinet when no one was around."

"You must have got your idea when everyone was interested in the lake monster," added Millie. "Then you stole the vegetables and sacks to make a fake creature, and you chose the turnips because they float. Dragging the pretend monster to the lake must have left those scrape marks on the muddy shore."

"I nearly got away with it too." Lord Dellwort's face twisted into a sneer. "But right from the start you girls were in my way. I went to the boathouse last night to hide the rest of the sacks and turnips and there you were — snooping around." He glared at Millie and Jess. "You two are the biggest pests in the palace!"

The queen took the necklace from Millie. "We trusted you," she said to Lord Dellwort. "You were here as our guest to see the festival."

"Who cares about the silly festival!" said Lord Dellwort scornfully. "I only came because I needed money. I could have sold that sapphire for a lot of gold coins."

The king rose to his feet, his face growing red. "Take him away!" he commanded, and the chief guard marched his lordship from the room.

"Dear me! It's all been much too exciting." Lady Snood dabbed her face with a lacy handkerchief before turning to Jess. "Would you mind getting me some of those delicious-sounding butterfly cakes? I think they'd be the perfect thing to calm my nerves."

Jess smiled. "I'll fetch them right away."

"I'll help you!" said Millie.

As Jess and Millie left the parlour, Lady Snood said to the queen, "Those girls are very smart and brave. They remind me of myself at that age!"

The people of Plumchester streamed

through the palace gates for the festival the next day. Autumn sunshine warmed the air and the leaves on the trees were starting to turn gold. Many people had brought along things for the competitions, but none of the cakes looked as good as Cook's, Jess thought.

Queen Belinda took Prince Edward to watch the performers on the croquet lawn. Violin players struck up a jig while dancers in bright costumes leapt and twirled to the music. The little prince giggled and clapped along. The queen smiled and touched the sparkling Sky Sapphire hanging round her neck.

Millie and Jess went down to the lake where Mr Steen was judging the fruit and vegetable stall, ready to hand out the prizes.

"Would you like some help, Mr Steen?" asked Jess.

The butler dismissed her with a wave of his skinny arm. "Go and enjoy yourself! Have a slice of Cook's wonderful chocolate cake. You deserve to have some fun and the *best* thing is there's no monster to ruin the day!"

Millie raised her eyebrows as they carried on walking. "Do you think he's feeling all right? He's never told you to have some fun before."

Jess grinned. "I think he's glad the creature in the lake was just pretend."

"I sort of wish it had been real. It would have been so exciting!" Millie stopped to throw a stone in the water. Ripples rolled outwards from where it landed.

A moment later, the reeds beside the bank started to rustle.

Millie clutched Jess's arm, hissing, "Something's in there!"

A soggy golden beast leapt out of the water carrying an oddly-shaped branch in his mouth.

"Jax, you made us jump!" exclaimed Jess. "Have you been making friends with the ducks again?"

Millie wrestled the branch out of the dog's mouth. "Look at this!" She turned the log over and showed Jess two dark hollows in the wood that seemed just like eyes. "It's the monster's head we saw in the water that misty day on the bridge. It was just a branch all the time!"

"It's strange how your eyes can trick you!" Jess smiled. "We should remember that when the next mystery comes along. Never trust what you see – not till you're absolutely sure."

"And never be scared of a turnip monster!" Millie linked arms with Jess and they climbed the hill to get a slice of Cook's wonderful chocolate cake.

Turn over for some fun
puzzles and quizzes – grab a
friend and play together!

Find the Sapphire!

Can you help Millie and Jess find the
missing necklace in the castle maze?

Start

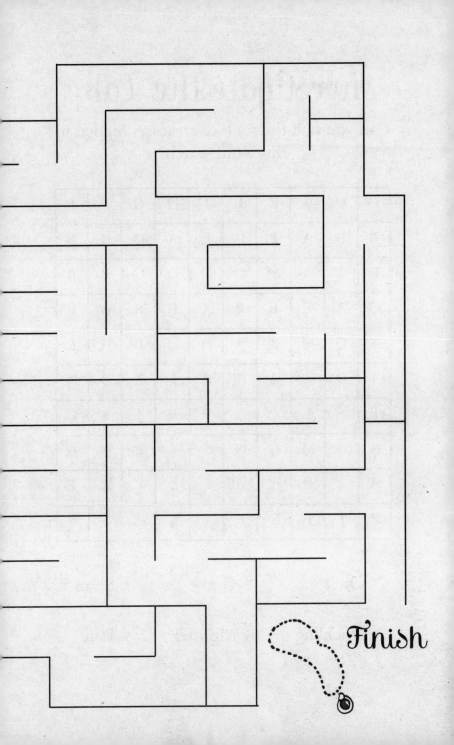

Finish

Investigate the Lake

Can you find the six lake creatures hidden in this word search?

D	U	C	K	L	I	N	G	F	F
P	B	A	E	G	E	A	O	K	B
D	I	A	M	O	N	D	O	P	A
O	A	E	E	P	X	E	S	W	P
T	Q	M	R	S	D	U	E	H	L
T	D	X	A	W	P	I	Z	D	H
E	S	I	L	A	V	E	J	A	U
R	U	M	O	N	S	T	E	R	A
A	T	B	H	B	S	E	V	R	E
Z	J	F	Y	F	I	S	H	I	L

✷ Otter   ✷ Goose   ✷ Swan

✷ Duckling   ✷ Monster   ✷ Fish

Who has been swimming in the lake?

Connect the dots to reveal
the lake creature…

Spot the difference

Can you spot the five differences?

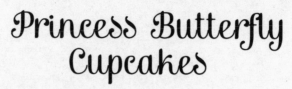

Princess Butterfly Cupcakes

After a day of solving mysteries, make some butterfly cakes using Jess and Millie's favourite recipe.

Ingredients

For the cake:

- 110g self-raising flour
- 110g caster sugar
- 110g butter/margarine
- 2 tsp baking powder
- 2 eggs

For the icing:

- 110g butter
- 220g icing sugar
- A tbsp of milk
- Sprinkles

Equipment

Bun tin, mixing bowl, wooden spoon, 12 cake cases, whisk.

- Ask a grown-up to preheat the oven to 180°C (fan)/200°C (electric)/Gas mark 6.
- Lay out 12 cake cases in a bun tin.
- Mix the sugar, flour and baking powder together.

- Add the butter/margarine and eggs.
- Whisk all of it together.
- Using a teaspoon, fill the cake cases with the mixture (be sure to give them an even amount each).
- Put the tray in the oven for 15 minutes, until they are golden brown.
- Take them out of the oven and let them cool.
- Make the icing by whisking the butter and sugar together with a spoon of milk, until it is light and fluffy.
- Use a knife (or ask a grown-up) to scoop a hole out of the top of the cake.
- Cut the scooped out cake in half. Fill the hole in the cake with icing and then place the cut out cake on top (like wings).
- Sprinkle some sprinkles on top of your cakes, and enjoy!

You must have an adult around to help you.

Here is a peek at the next Tiara
Friends adventure...

Chapter One

The Artist of Bodkin Street

Jess dashed up the back stairs of Peveril Palace. Her white apron was smudged with sooty fingerprints and her mob cap was falling over one ear. She knocked on the door to Princess Amelia's chamber before bursting in.

"Millie!" she gasped. "Your mother sent me to fetch you. The carriage is waiting to take you to Plumchester."

Princess Amelia (called Millie, for short) swung round, holding one hand to her neck. The two girls were the same age and they looked so much alike that they could have been twins. They both had glossy brown hair that curled over their shoulders, small noses and hazel eyes. The only difference between them was that Jess's eyes were a little darker.

They'd been best friends ever since Jess came to Peveril Palace to work as a maid. They loved looking the same and they secretly called themselves Double Trouble!

"I can't go to Plumchester!" cried Millie. "Mother wants me to have my portrait painted by that new artist in Bodkin Street."

"Don't you want to have your picture painted?" asked Jess.

"It's not that – look!" Millie took her hand away from her neck and showed Jess a bright yellow stain across her skin. "I put on face paints last night – I was pretending to be a lion in the jungle. I washed most of it off before I went to bed but I must have missed this bit and now I can't get rid of it. Mother will be so cross! She warned me not to make a mess."

Jess grinned. "I bet you looked great as a lion. Can't you put on a silk scarf to hide the mark?"

"I know Mother won't let me. She's already decided exactly what I should wear. The portrait's going to be a present for Grandmother in Glenbarr so it has to be perfect." Millie pulled a face.

"Why don't we swap places? I'll get my picture painted and you can finish my chores. No one will ever know!" Jess's eyes twinkled. She and Millie swapped places all the time so that they could both do their favourite things. Jess would go to Millie's horse-riding lesson while Millie went to the palace kitchen to bake cakes with Cook Walsh. It was pretty awesome to be a maid and a princess all in one day!

Millie clapped her hands excitedly. "I'd love to swap! But are you sure you don't mind?"

Jess grinned. "Course not! We'd better hurry though. What do I have to wear?"

Millie went to her big wooden wardrobe and took out a long purple dress with sparkly beads all over the top and a silver sash around the waist. Jess took off her maid uniform and gave it to Millie, before pulling the dress over her white petticoat.

Millie put the maid dress on and fastened the apron round her waist. Then she brushed Jess's long hair until it hung beautifully over her shoulders before clipping an emerald necklace round her friend's neck.

Jess gazed into the large gold-framed mirror and her heart skipped. She was used to wearing royal clothes but this was one of Millie's finest dresses which was only worn on very special occasions.

"You look great!" Millie beamed. "Are you all right? Is the dress too scratchy?"

"It's fine! You'd better take this." Jess picked up her mob cap and put it on Millie's head. "I hope Mr Steen doesn't give you too many chores."

"Don't worry about me—" Millie broke off at the sound of footsteps.

There was a sharp knock on the door. "Come in!" the girls called together.

Mr Steen, the royal butler, opened the door, his eyebrows lowered in disapproval. "You were meant to fetch the princess right away, Jess," he said to Millie. "The royal carriage is waiting."

"Sorry, Mr Steen." Millie turned away to hide a giggle.

"Here!" Jess handed her friend a gauzy white scarf and stared meaningfully at the stain on Millie's skin. "This will keep your neck warm."

"Oh! Thank you." Millie wrapped it

round her neck to hide the yellow mark.

Jess felt a fluttering in her stomach as she followed the butler downstairs. Riding out in the royal carriage wearing a special dress and an emerald necklace seemed very daring. As she sat down in the carriage, she noticed one of the gardeners leaning on his spade and staring through a window into the banquet hall.

Just then Mr Larum, Millie's teacher, rushed down the steps carrying a large package wrapped in brown paper and string. "I'm ready!" he gasped as he climbed into the carriage. "And I've got the royal paintings."

"You there!" Mr Steen spotted the gardener leaning on his spade. "You're new here, aren't you? Aren't there some flower beds that need digging?"

"Yes, sir. I'm sorry." The gardener pulled

his straw hat down low and hurried away.

The coachman called to the horses and the carriage rolled forward. Jess watched the royal lake and the golden palace gates go by. Then they were rumbling down the street towards the city of Plumchester.

Mr Larum sat opposite Jess holding the wrapped-up paintings carefully. King James had noticed their frames needed mending so he'd asked Mr Larum to take them to the artist in Bodkin Street who would surely know how to fix them.

"There is such a lot of history behind these paintings," said Mr Larum, straightening his dark-rimmed glasses. "They were painted more than a hundred years ago during the reign of King Ned, your great-grandfather."

Jess smiled and tried to listen but there were so many exciting things outside the window. Street sellers were setting out

stalls with everything from fruit to feather hats. Halfpenny Square, where the biggest market was held, was filling with people and noise.

As the carriage rolled along, Jess tried to remember one thing about each person she saw — the lace on a lady's sleeves or the colour of a man's coat. It was something she'd been practising in case it came in handy for solving mysteries.

She and Millie had solved quite a few puzzles lately. It had all begun when Prince Edward's little diamond crown went missing right before his first birthday. The two girls had searched for clues and found the crown. Jess couldn't help wondering whether there was another mystery out there, waiting to be discovered.

At last, the carriage turned left and drew to a stop in Bodkin Street. Jess flung the carriage door open and jumped down, quite forgetting to let the coachman open it for her like a princess should. She loved Bodkin Street. She'd lived here in her parents' dressmaking shop, Buttons and Bows, before becoming a maid at the palace. She knew every house and shop in the lane, except the exciting new artist's studio.

Smiling, she waved to Miss Clackton, the kind but scatty owner of the Pet Emporium next door to her parents' shop. The Pet Emporium was a place for pampering pets and was filled with every kind of animal toy and treat Jess could think of.

The wonderful smell of freshly baked cakes drifted out of Mr Bibby's bakery just across the road. Next door to the bakery was the ironmonger's and Mr Heddon, who ran the shop, was sweeping the doorstep.

"This way, Princess Amelia." The

coachman beckoned her towards a bright red front door. *Gilbert Small's Studio* was painted in gold letters on a sign above the window.

Jess stepped forward eagerly. Mr Gilbert Small was the only person in Bodkin Street that she'd never met. It was only two weeks since he'd moved in and set up his artist studio and this was Jess's first chance to look inside! A proper painter like Mr Small must be very serious and probably frowned a lot while trying to get his pictures just right.

The coachman held the door and Mr Larum staggered inside with his package of paintings. Following him, Jess gazed around with wide eyes. Tall trees with dangling tropical fruit were painted across the walls. Pictures of birds with bright feathers and monkeys with furry faces peeped from the painted branches. Dazzling flowers in magenta, gold and crimson were drawn on the forest floor. Overhead, the ceiling was a beautiful shade of blue.

Jess caught her breath. It was like stepping into a jungle.

"Welcome, welcome!" boomed a large man with ginger hair and a beard. He shook Mr Larum's hand. "Nice to see you, sir! And this must be the princess."

"Hello!" Jess tried not to stare as she curtsied. How could someone called Mr Small be so enormous? He was like a ginger-haired giant.

Mr Larum unwrapped the parcel of paintings and began talking to Gilbert Small about the repairs, so Jess looked around the room. Paintings of places and people were stacked against the walls. Beside a large easel was a chair with a sleepy ginger cat lying on it. Jess peeked at the paper on the easel but it was blank.

"I'll let you get on." Mr Larum shook the artist's hand again. "I'll be back with the carriage at midday."

Mr Small stacked the royal pictures that Mr Larum had brought carefully to one side. Then he stroked the sleeping ginger cat. "Rumble-tum! You're sitting on the young lady's chair. This is Rumble-tum," he told Jess. "I gave him that name because he purrs so loudly."

Rumble-tum yawned and stretched, before climbing down.

"Will it take you long to paint me, Mr Small?" Jess asked timidly as she sat down on the chair.

"Call me Gilbert!" he boomed, lines creasing round his eyes as he smiled. "No, it won't take too long. Now sit as comfortably as you can and I'll start the picture."

Jess tried to sit very still but she jumped

when Rumble-tum sprang on to her knees. She stroked the cat's fluffy ginger ears and he curled up on her lap, purring loudly. Jess smiled. "I think Rumble-tum wants to be in the picture too!"